Written by Benji Bennett.
benji@adamscloud.com

Illustrations by Roxanne Burchartz.
Roxanneburchartz@gmail.com

Designed by Bold.
www.reallybold.com

First UK edition 2016 printed in Ireland by Watermans Printers
www.watermansprinters.ie

ISBN: 978-1-906818-10-4

Published by

An imprint of Adam's Printing Press Publishing.

Adam's Cloud is dedicated to spreading Adam's message of the importance of love, laughter and play within the family
and will make a donation from the proceeds of all books published under its imprint to children's charities.

Adam's Cloud
PO Box 11379, Blackrock, Co. Dublin, Ireland.
Email: info@adamscloud.com
Web: www.adamscloud.com
Tel: +353 1 2833620

2% of the proceeds from the sale of this book will go to

Barretstown's mission is to rebuild the lives of children affected by serious illness, and their families, through a life changing therapeutic
recreation programme in a safe, fun and supportive environment. Barretstown provides a carefree, challenging and healing experience which
deals with the emotional effects of a child's illness – creating a profound and positive impact on their lives – with lasting results.
Barretstown was founded in 1994, by the late Paul Newman and is a SeriousFun Camp.

It's time to sleep but before you go

there's something I really want you to know...

I love you much more than
a big sandy beach,

with sand dunes so high
they seem far out of reach.

I love you much more than
the things that we've made,

on a hot sunny day
with our bucket and spade.

To build a castle
from sand would be great,

with seaweed for a roof
and sea shells for a gate.

We could run to the rocks
and could use them as blocks,

and for a flag on the top
we could use someone's socks.

I love you much more than a big sandy beach

I love you much more than
the sun, moon and stars,

even much more than
the red planet Mars.

I love you much more than
the outer space tune,

sung to the world
by the man on the moon.

I love you much more than the sun, moon and stars

If we could fly in a big rocket ship,
what fun we would have
on our magical trip.

We could speed through the clouds
to the heavens above

and tell outer space aliens
all about love.

I love you much more than
the burning bright sun,

I love it so much
when we play and have fun.

I love you much more
than the world's tallest trees,

even much more
than a hug and a squeeze.

I love you much

If we were a bee think of all we could see,

as we fly to the top
of the world's tallest tree.

We could fly all around the daisies and roses,

floating on the air
with sweet smells for our noses.

nore than the burning bright sun

I love you much more than
the deepest blue sea.

I love you so much
when you swim beside me.

I love you much more than
the sea's octopuses,

going to school on their
submarine buses.

I love you much mor

If we could sail on a big pirate's ship,
we could walk the long plank
and take a quick dip.

How great it would be
to find us some treasure,

made up of toys
that would be such a pleasure.

than the deepest blue sea

I love you much more than
the world's biggest plane,

that could fly us up high
and away from the rain.

I love you so much when
I hold your sweet hand,

as we speed through the air
to a far away land.

...an the world's biggest plane

To fly round the world
in a big jumbo jet,

would be a great trip
that we'd never forget.

High up in the skies
we'd get such a surprise,

to see wonderful things
with our very own eyes.

I love you much more than
a big dinosaur,

that ruled over the Earth
with his big scary roar.

I love you much more than
a big grizzly bear,

who could scare a T-Rex
with a very cross stare.

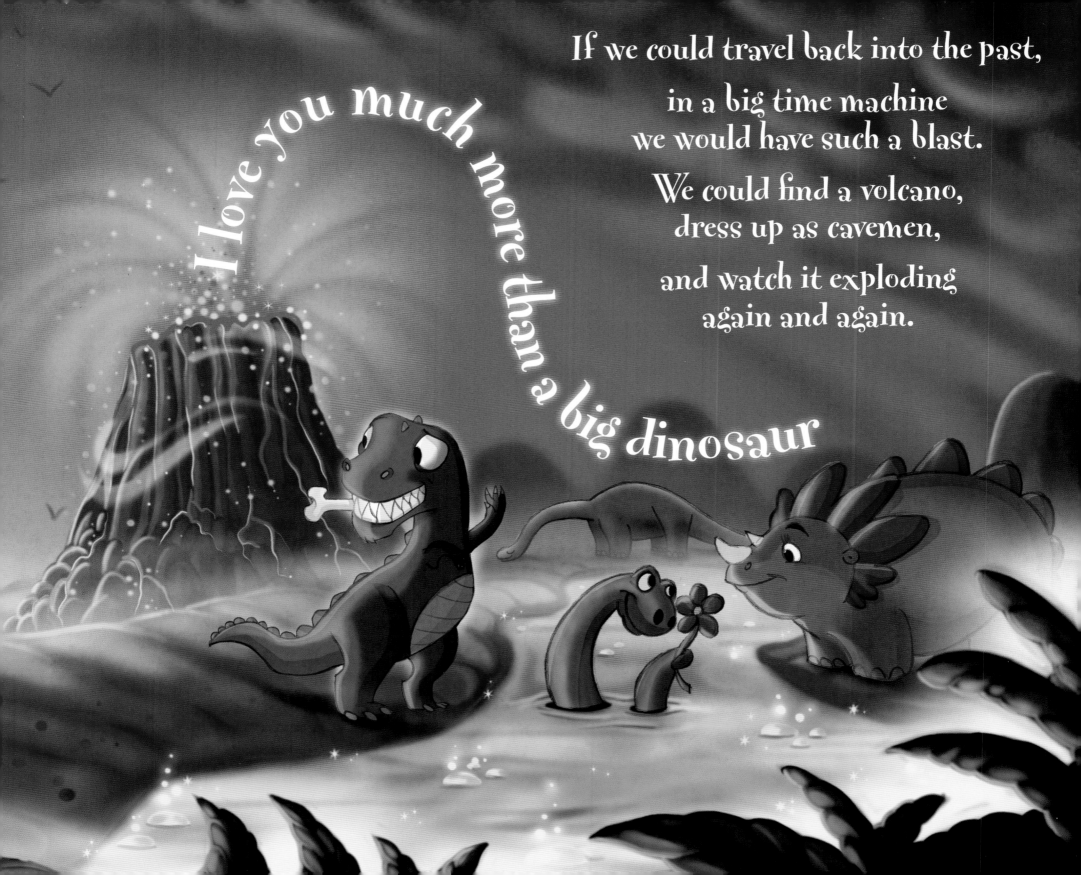

I love you much more than a big dinosaur

If we could travel back into the past,
in a big time machine
we would have such a blast.

We could find a volcano,
dress up as cavemen,
and watch it exploding
again and again.

I love you much more than
a Halloween night,

when we dress up as ghosts
and give people a fright.

I love you much more than
a witch loves her broom,

mixing up potions in her
spell-making room.

I love you much more than a Halloween night

If we could dress up and do trick-or-treats,
we could fill up our bag with some nuts and some sweets.

We could light a candle in a big pumpkin's head
and eat some of our sweets before we went to bed.

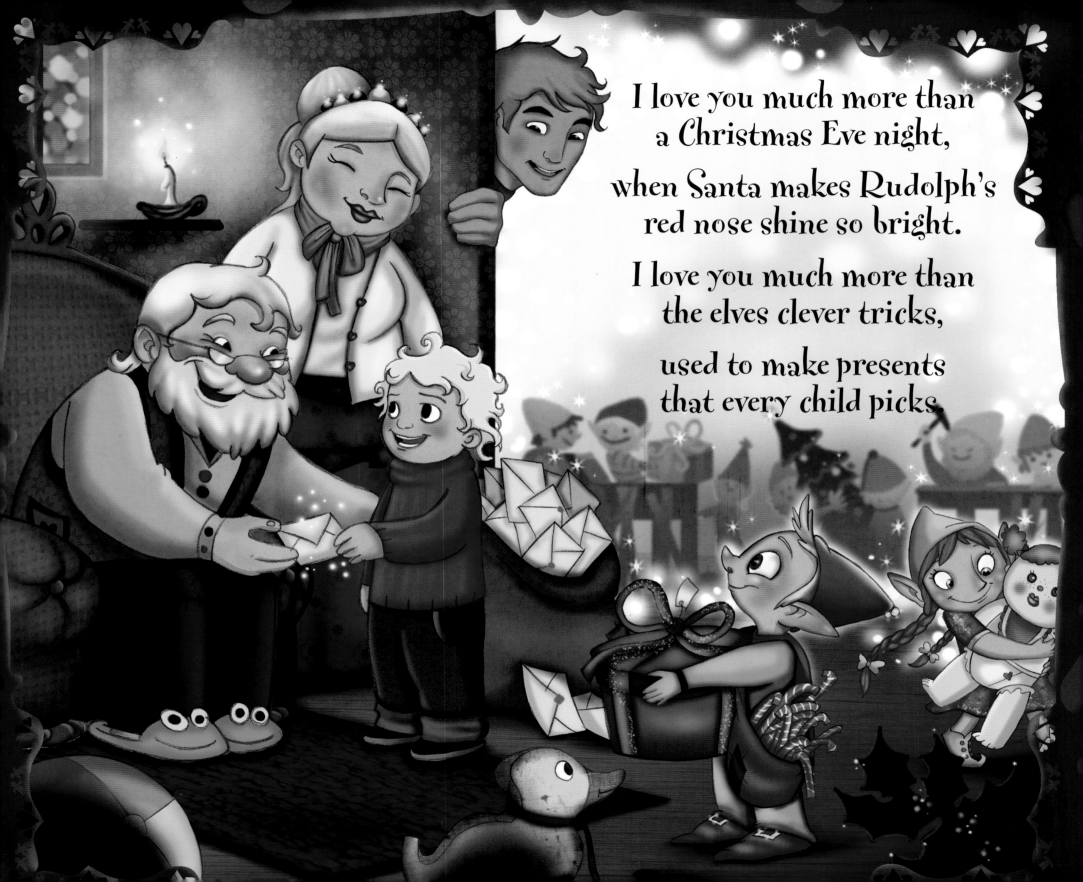

I love you much more than
a Christmas Eve night,

when Santa makes Rudolph's
red nose shine so bright.

I love you much more than
the elves clever tricks,

used to make presents
that every child picks.

I love you much more than a Christmas Eve night

If we could fly to the North Pole and land,
we could deliver our letter to Santa by hand.

We could help all the elves load up Santa's sleigh
and wave to the reindeers as they fly away.

I love you much more than the world's biggest truck,
picking up boulders and scooping up muck.

I love you much more than red dynamite,
that makes a big bang with red flashes of light.

I love you much more than th

If I drove a crane
and you drove a digger,

we could both work together
to make mountains bigger.

We could dress up as builders
with bright yellow hats,

and build some apartments
for eagles and bats.

world's biggest truck

I love you much more than the world's biggest slide,
even much more than a rollercoaster ride.

I love you much more than a big theme parade,
with singing and dancing as sweet music played.

I love you much mor

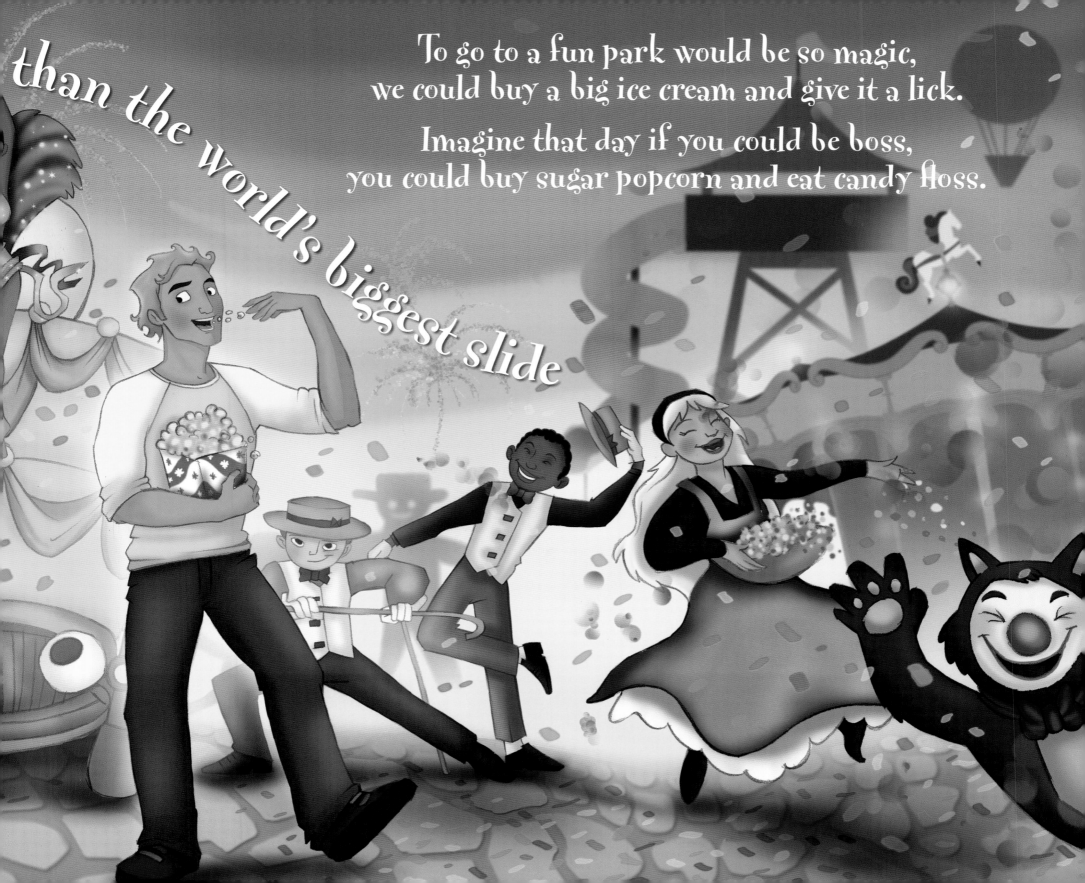

than the world's biggest slide

To go to a fun park would be so magic,
we could buy a big ice cream and give it a lick.

Imagine that day if you could be boss,
you could buy sugar popcorn and eat candy floss.

The person who loves you so much like no other,
is the person that loves you the most and your Mother.
She loves you so much 'coz you grew in her tummy,
and that is why she is your wonderful Mummy.

Night, Night

Night, night, sleep tight my bundle of joy,
I love you much more than my favourite toy.
My love for you is as bright as sunlight.
Sweet dreams, my love, I bid you good night.

leep tight my bundle of joy